THE ADVENTURE OF THE TORN FOUNDERS

From the casebook of

Dr John H Watson

To Holmes she was always *the* child. For the most part he avoided the company of children - the only exceptions being his Baker Street Irregulars, one or more of whom occasionally graced our sitting room at 221b, sitting to attention on the sofa as he detailed the warehouse, barge or hackney carriage he desired them to find. Even here he would converse with them as though little adults, his benevolence restricted to a mere word of praise if a task was successfully completed and to the ubiquitous half-crown payment that was the usual going rate for each boy. It was their invisibility to the worlds they inhabited, and hence their usefulness as spies, that was their sole attraction for him. It would have been unthinkable for him to ruffle the hair on one or consider a little game with another. However, whenever (after the events I am about to relate) he met Caroline - admittedly still an infrequent occurrence - he would transform into an indulgent, avuncular, almost playful figure that was as alien to me as his pipe and violin were familiar.

The episode started, as so often, with the two of us in our rooms in Baker Street. It was a late afternoon in early December and the weather was deciding whether to shroud the city in fog or snow. Both had been much in evidence in the last week and the view from our first floor window was of a swirling grey vapour diffused with the yellow iridescence of the street lamps and merging below with the whiter street. Distances were impossible to judge. The sounds of an occasional carriage or the hurried footsteps of a passing pedestrian were muffled almost into silence. A fire burnt in our grate and Holmes was standing in one of his characteristic, though unaffected poses just to one side of it puffing busily at his long, curved churchwarden pipe. The atmosphere in the room was somewhat close owing to his having spent much of the afternoon curled in his favourite armchair wrapped in his old dressing gown, eyes half-closed, holding a newspaper cutting and letting smoke curl upwards from the self-same pipe upon which he was currently drawing. I knew him too well to ask what particular problem he was pondering. When in one of these apparent trances he would respond to interruptions either not at all or with a curt, irritated bark leaving both parties in a poor temper.

But now, as he had risen from his seat and was regarding the room with an expression of equanimity I judged it safe to assume that his train of thought had come to some conclusion and his unique brain could be persuaded to enter into more mundane channels of social discourse.

'Was that cutting the final clue in some great mystery that you have now solved from the comfort of your armchair?' I asked, only half in jest.

He looked up from his labours with his pipe, seeing me as if for the first time in days although we had been closeted together all afternoon, and then smiled.

'Hardly, my dear Watson,' he replied. 'Simply one of those curious little incidents that occurs from time to time in a city and that are beloved of newspapers to flesh out the spaces between the larger news items. But as you know, it is those quirkier sides of life that hold an especial appeal for me in my line of work. Take a look: what do you make of it?'

He held out the clipping to me. It was an article of two columns neatly cut out of yesterday's Gazette. The heading was immediately arresting: "THREE NOBLEMEN ATTACKED IN ST JAMES".

'Good heavens, Holmes!' I cried. 'This is outrageous! These villains must be brought to justice!'

Holmes smiled indulgently. 'Your concern and indignation do you credit, Watson. But before you become too agitated - read on. I have told you before that it is a capital mistake to theorise without the facts.'

Somewhat nettled, I picked up the cutting, which I had thrown upon the table in my shock at reading the headline, and settled myself in an armchair to read the article.

As the Yuletide festivities are all but upon us we are to expect some high spirits and perhaps the more than liberal consumption of alcohol in certain quarters but yesterday some of these premature celebrations took on a deplorable turn as the portraits of no fewer than three venerable aristocrats, hanging in the smoking rooms of their St James clubs, were vandalised.

Over the space of two hours the same sequence had repeated itself at the East India, the Army & Navy and the Travellers Clubs. Members reported a window being broken with a sharp crack and, upon investigating, no one to be seen in the admittedly fog-bound street. When returning their attentions to the rooms they found in each case that the missile that had fractured the glass panes had passed through the room and, with unerring accuracy, defaced a portrait by the tearing of a gash in the canvas. On the floor beneath the ruined pictures was always found a champagne cork from bottles of varying vintages.

The portraits were in each case half-length oil portraits of their subjects and of considerable value, although their sentimental and historical value to each club was incalculably higher. Sir William Grafton, chairman of the East India club - the first building thus attacked - said: 'This sort of mindless hooliganism is symptomatic of the liberal attitudes towards the criminal classes so prevalent today. We are engaging London's foremost picture restorer to see if the damage to our prized portrait of Prince Albert can be repaired. Meantime we look to Scotland Yard to track down the perpetrators and bring the full force of the law to bear on them.

The sentence meted out should act as a deterrent to future generations of vandals.'

The other portraits attacked were of Lieutenant General Sir Edward Barnes at the Army & Navy Club and the Earl of Aberdeen at the Travellers.

Inspector Lestrade of the Yard, more usually employed in the solving of high-profile murder cases, has been drafted into this investigation at the request of several well-connected members of the three clubs concerned and last night announced that an arrest had already been made. A vagrant who had for some time been sleeping rough in the central gardens of St James Square was apprehended. In his makeshift shelter under a bush in a corner of the garden several other bottles of intoxicating liquor were found. Apparently he had been resident there for some time, accessing the gardens after dark by scaling the iron railings - the gates being locked at dusk.

Our sympathies are extended to the members of the three institutions concerned, for having their preparations for the festive season so deplorably interrupted.

I looked up. Holmes was regarding me keenly. He raised an inquiring eyebrow. 'Well? An intriguing little problem, don't you think?'

'Well, I wouldn't call it intriguing. A downright disgrace. I know that portrait for I am a member of the East India club. Let us hope the vagabond is securely locked up for a lengthy spell. If respect for property is not ingrained it must be drilled into the fellow.'

'My dear chap!' retorted Holmes. 'Do you mean to tell me that you cannot see the developing mystery in that article?'

'I see nothing other than an outrage committed by a wastrel.'

'On the contrary, Watson. You see everything but deduce nothing. There is more here than meets the eye.' He chuckled. 'Lestrade has really surpassed himself this time by arresting the vagrant. Still, I suppose he'll be glad of a warm cell for a day or two whilst the strings unravel. It is particularly inclement weather - even for this time of year.' He puffed away at his pipe again, which was on the point of extinguishing.

'What can you mean, Holmes?' I cried. 'Do you see a different solution to all this? How?'

His pipe bowl now glowing brightly he regarded me through a cloud of smoke. 'You know my methods - apply them.'

'I confess I am at a loss to know what else you could read into this. Even if the fellow is not guilty one could not tell that from the information given here.'

'Tut, Watson! Can you not see the objections to the arrest at least, even you fail to grasp the wider possibilities of the case?'

'The arrest? But the man was caught living in the Square's gardens and had bottles of alcohol all around him!' I exclaimed.

Holmes looked severe. 'Being of insufficient means to afford a lodging is not yet a crime, Watson. The case against him is purely circumstantial. And in any case, should the man acquire a few pennies, do you imagine he would spend them on a champagne bottle?'

'He might have stolen them,' I countered obstinately although I knew he was right.

'If so, they would all have been of the same type - he could hardly steal them piecemeal,' Holmes retorted irritably. 'And even then he would have rather drunk them in his hide-out.'

I pondered this. 'I see what you mean. If he had thrown something it would have been a beer bottle.'

'Not even that. Alcohol has too high a value for someone like him to be employed as a missile. A stone would suffice - surely?'

'Quite true, Holmes,' I agreed. 'What else has caught your eye? The locations of the clubs perhaps?'

'That is suggestive, certainly,' he responded. 'Again, the tramp would not venture as far from his temporary domicile as Pall Mall in order to vent his spleen by throwing an object. He would stay in the square. No - the distribution is too wide to be put down to a fit of drunken rage. In any case it is too cold for him to have been anywhere but huddling under whatever rags he has accumulated, not wandering around the streets. The man in Lestrade's cells may yet have a valuable part to play in this drama - but as a witness, not a suspect.'

'You think he may have seen the real culprit?'

'It is possible. I am sure he would have been within the Square's garden and hence may have had a view of the first attack through the railings if he wasn't asleep or already drunk. I hope to be able to question him when Lestrade realises his error.'

'And when will he do that?'

'When the next attack occurs.'

'What!' I was stunned. 'You think there will be more?'

'I think it not unlikely. If we allow that the vagrant was not the perpetrator of the crime and that it was more than simply a random act of destruction then there must have been a purpose - and that has not yet been revealed. No theft, no murder, nothing else has occurred other than this singular trio of paintings having been damaged. No, no - it won't do, Watson. There is a deeper game afoot here. Yes, this promises to be a most interesting case.'

'Your reasoning is, as ever, so logical. Marvelous, Holmes!'

'Commonplace, Watson. Commonplace.'

'Shouldn't you tell Lestrade?'

'I am not retained by the police to sort out their mistakes. In any case I do not yet know where the next assault is planned.'

My head was spinning by this stage as always when I tried to keep up with the furious pace of Holmes' brain. I had by now grasped the improbability of the tramp having fired the champagne corks - that was easy enough when explained - but how had Holmes deduced the rest? He had, it seemed to me access to no more information than I yet I could make no further progress.

'What else have you made of it?'

But Holmes sprang out of the chair on which he had been watching my feeble efforts at deduction and strode for the hall. 'No time for that, Watson!' he cried. 'We must make haste if we are to procure some champagne before the shop closes for the night.'

'A celebration?'

'An experiment, my dear fellow. We need at least three bottles and then I propose to open them in a warehouse in the docks which I know to be unused currently. Then we might be in a position to enlighten Lestrade. The venture does entail a little law-breaking: are you game?'

For a moment I feared that my friend had been at the seven percent solution again and was displaying the ill effects that will befall any addict eventually but one look at the expression on his keen, angular face was sufficient to convince me that he was truly on a scent and in full control of his faculties.

'Would you like me to come along?' It was all I could do to keep the hope put of my voice.

'Essential, Watson. Essential,' he replied already half into his overcoat and searching for his gloves. 'The experiment needs two.'

*

The cold as we left the building was of that raw, bone-chilling type that seems to go right through you. I shivered and drew my thick ulster closer round me. Holmes, who seemed as impervious to temperature as to hunger, smiled at me.

'If you were a tramp who had ensconced himself in a makeshift shelter of blankets and sticks would you venture forth in this to throw stones at random windows?'

'I see what you mean, Holmes,' I replied. 'No, the more I think of the poor fellow in his camp the more I think he has been wronged.'

We walked through a thin layer of snow to the corner of Baker Street towards Portman Square, where there was a shop that was well stocked with all manner of wines. From a distance we saw its welcome glow through the fog and I was relieved when we were inside so that I could take advantage of the warmth. Holmes however was not disposed to linger for once he was on a case he was indefatigable and seemed to possess boundless energy. He laid two sovereigns on the counter whilst the short proprietor, having satisfied himself that we were bona fide customers, bustled about fetching a selection of champagnes. Holmes simply picked the first three bottles and turned on his heel leaving an astonished shopkeeper behind counting the considerable change into his own pocket.

Outside in the cold wet fog he looked about for a Hackney carriage. We had to wait some minutes for traffic was sparse in such weather, even in as central a location as ours but eventually one arrived and we climbed inside. Holmes gave the address of his disused warehouse in a part of the East End of which I had never heard, much less visited. How he came to acquire the nuggets of information with which he stacked his cerebral attic I did not know but the store of London-related data was immense.

'Why are we going to this place?' I asked. 'And what on earth is this experiment you wish to undertake?'

Holmes leaned back in the carriage, brought his gloved fingertips together in front of his lips and thought awhile.

'Consider the facts, Watson. In each case a pane of glass is shattered, at an angle for the portraits hung on the walls, and each time an unerring direct hit is scored on the painting in question. Does that not strike you as odd?'

'Clearly the culprit had an excellent aim,' I said. A thought struck me. 'Perhaps with marksmanship like that we should be seeking a military man?'

Holmes chuckled. 'Indeed? With marksmanship like that we should seek a magician!'

'What can you mean?'

'All in good time, dear Doctor,' he replied. 'But let us move on. Consider the effect of the missile. Do you recall?'

Proudly I recollected the paragraph. 'Each time a gash was torn into the canvass.'

Holmes smirked. 'By a *cork*?'

'Perhaps the wire cage that secures the cork to the bottle was left on. Travelling at speed that would cause considerable damage to whatever it struck.' I was pleased with my reasoning.

'And lend even more aerodynamic stability to the object, I suppose? Do you really mean to tell me that the cork could be fired at an angle to the window towards the painting, smash the glass and continue on its intended path whilst not deviating an inch and then, each time, hit the canvass with the edge of the wire cage? No, no, Watson. It stretches credibility beyond breaking point.'

I had to admit that, told in this way, he had a point.

'And there is a further, even more serious objection,' he added.

'What?'

'That is what our experiment will demonstrate.'

After that I could not draw him any further on the subject. He closed his eyes, oblivious to the cold that seeped through the carriage doors. I shivered.

*

'Wait for us here, cabby' said Holmes as we alighted in a dark, deserted, grubby street near the docks. The man looked doubtful despite the sovereign that Holmes had placed in his hand. Clearly he did not relish the area in which we found ourselves nor was fully confident of our return. He looked wistfully at the gold coin.

'I'll tell you what,' said Holmes, taking a five-pound note from his notebook and tearing it in half, giving half to the astounded driver. When we return - and we shall do so inside fifteen minutes - then you get the other half of this. Then you can buy your good lady something to make amends for this morning. So - will you wait?'

The cabby looked at Holmes in awe. 'Now 'ow do you know my misses and me had a tiff this morning?'

'It's my business to know things other people don't,' replied Holmes and without further ado set off down the street in the direction of the river.

'How on earth did you know about his argument?' I wanted to know.

'Tut, Watson. You have no children yet but when you do and I see you arrive at work with a smear of your child's breakfast on the shoulder of your ulster I shall know that you had to wind the infant instead of your wife just as you were setting off. Whilst this could mean that your wife was ill, in that situation you would not have had on your coat. More likely you were forced into the manoeuvre when she disappeared upstairs after the disagreement. But when in addition to this I notice a bunch of flowers beside you then I know you are bringing home a peace offering.'

'Masterful!' I exclaimed.

'Elementary,' he replied.

At the end of the street he turned left into an alleyway that seemed to lead straight to the bank of the river. One or two lights on the prows of the barges moored close to the shore winked through the gloom. About halfway down this turning there loomed a large structure behind a rickety fence - Holmes' abandoned warehouse. He felt his way along until he found a pair of loose planks that swung easily aside to allow is to scramble through into the grounds. Weeds grew in abundance as testament to the building's disused status. Holmes carrying two of the champagne bottles, one in each hand, walked round the outside until he found what he had evidently being seeking.

'Here we are, Watson. Behold our targets!' He waved a hand at the ground floor windows, about half of which remained unbroken.

'You want us to break these windows with champagne corks?' I asked as the true intent of our journey began to dawn on me. 'Why?'

'You shall see. I need to prove to myself what I feel I know. Now Doctor: could you oblige me by firing your cork at this window here?' He indicated an intact pane. 'From a few feet away - to represent the width of a pavement. Give it a good shake first.'

Feeling both foolish and unnerved I did as I was bade. Then, removing the foil around the cork I loosened the wire cage and felt the cork straining against the building pressure in the bottle. As it began to ease out with no help from myself I aimed the bottle at the window like a rifle. A moment later with a loud rapport the cork with its wire casing shot out of the bottle and crashed into the window leaving me holding the opened bottle with champagne flooding out over my hands.

Holmes was instantly examining the smashed pane. When he turned round, even through the murky fog I could sense a triumphant gleam in his eyes.

'Excellent shot, Watson,' he said handing over the two bottles he had been carrying. 'Now this time a little closer and aim at this pane.' He indicated the adjacent one. I obliged and repeated the procedure, again hitting my target with similar results. Again Holmes bent over the resulting shards. A third and even closer shot followed shortly afterwards. Holmes straightened up after again picking something from the ground. He was smiling broadly.

'The value of imagination, my dear chap!' he cried. 'We formulate a hypothesis, test it and find the police sadly lacking.'

'But Holmes!' I protested, my hands becoming colder by the minute covered as they were in sparkling wine, 'what is it that you have learnt? I can dimly perceive that you were trying to re-enact the crime but to what end?

As an answer he held out his gloved fist and unclenched it revealing the three champagne corks.

'You were a excellent shot, Watson, but even at close range and firing upon windows doubtless of an inferior quality to those of the St James clubs, your cork could only break the panes - not travel through them. You would have had a hard time trying to damage anything inside the building. I think we need to look elsewhere for the source of the damage to the paintings. The corks are but a blind.'

'Look where, Holmes?'

'Inside the clubs themselves of course! Come on Watson - let us unite our faithful cabby with the other half of his five pound note before he gives up on us for it is a long walk back to Baker Street!'

*

By the time we regained our rooms it was late. Holmes had
been quiet during the return journey, presumably pondering
the implications of his experiment. Mrs Hudson had kept the
fire burning and I hunched over it still with my coat on, as I
was fair chilled to the marrow. Not so Holmes, who had
flung off his outer garments and was ranging our shelves in
search of a book. Our supper stood on the table but until I
had properly warmed up nothing would move me from in
front of the fireplace, even though I had not eaten since
lunchtime and I was famished.

'What book are you seeking?' I asked when some of the
warmth had begun to return to my body. 'I confess I am
again completely in the dark. If the man outside with the
corks did not ruin the portraits then who else could it have
been?'

'As to the identity of the man I too am ignorant but this
afternoon has been most profitable as to knowing where to
seek him.'

'Eight pounds would seem a little extravagant to confirm
what you presumably had expected to find, Holmes.'

'On the contrary, Watson. You are correct in saying that I
had my suspicions but they are nothing without proof - and
proof we now have. My eight pounds have bought me the
knowledge of where to look. The police continue to fumble
about in the streets of St James - if they are even looking at
all that is - whilst we know to suspect members of the three
clubs. The ideas are poles apart and hold the key to solving
this case. I would call that money well spent.'

'I suppose so,' I conceded somewhat reluctantly. Then a thought struck me. 'It could also be guests of members of the clubs,' I added, pleased to be able to steal a march on my friend for once.

'No, not guests. It is inconceivable that a non-member could be a guest at all three clubs in the space of two hours. One - yes, but we seek someone who is probably a member of at least two of the three establishments attacked.'

He laughed at my crestfallen expression and as if to cheer me, went on. 'Consider, Watson. A further attack this evening would narrow the field further if it were in a fourth venue.'

'You really think that is likely?'

'I think it is not improbable.'

We sat down to supper after our long afternoon in the cold and made a hearty meal of the cold pheasant that Mrs Hudson had left for us. With a couple of glasses of claret inside me I felt more like my old self. Holmes was able to switch off from a case completely whilst he awaited events and he discoursed widely upon the architecture of Whitehall, new regulations affecting shipping in the Port of London and the forthcoming production of Rigoletto at the Royal Opera House. It never ceased to amaze me how he could acquire such a wide yet thorough knowledge.

At the end of the meal I was feeling pleasantly drowsy but it was still too early to retire so I lay back in an armchair and not even Holmes scraping his bow aimlessly across the violin laid on his lap could arrest my slide into a doze. The fire crackled comfortingly in the hearth and the scent of pipe tobacco drifting across the room added to the soporific backdrop.

A violent hammering on the front door followed by Mrs Hudson's hurried footsteps to answer it dragged me sharply back to the present. I sat up. Holmes laid the fiddle on the floor by his chair and stretched out his feet.

'Lestrade,' he said.

'How could you possibly know that?'

'Clearly there has been another attack and his tramp theory has crumbled to pieces. Who else would venture out on a night like this and at this late hour?'

Moments later it was indeed Lestrade who burst into the room. 'Mr Holmes!' he cried. 'I am sorry to disturb you so late but I am at my wits' end and -'

'You wish to consult me about the fourth damaged portrait now that you have discovered that you arrested the wrong man yesterday and have had to release the St James Square vagrant. The considerable powers of Clubland are pressing you for answers. Where, pray, was tonight's incident?'

Lestrade stared at him as a child might at a magician after the production of a rabbit from a hat. 'Mr Holmes, this is beyond all explanation! How could you possibly know so exactly what has happened?'

'Simply following a logical train of though, Lestrade,' he replied. 'Now where did the attack occur?'

Lestrade looked reluctant to leave the matter of Holmes' prescience but quickly realised that there was a more pressing issue at stake.

'The London Library,' he replied. 'Just one hour ago the same incident occurred as yesterday. A champagne cork was fired from the street, broke a window and tore into the large portrait of Thomas Carlyle that hangs in the front study. Only a few members were present in the room at the time and they rushed to the window immediately but saw no one outside.'

'My, my,' said Holmes. 'St James Square is becoming a very unsafe neighbourhood. What have you done so far?'

'Well, there is nothing I can do, is there? There was no one in the square and I cannot for the life of me see why someone would want to damage paintings by firing missiles at them in this usually sedate corner of London.'

'You've done nothing!' exclaimed Holmes, horrified. 'Good heavens man - how many clues do you need to start to act?'

'But there are no clues, Mr Holmes!' wailed the inspector.

'So far I can count seven - but I haven't inspected the scene of the crime yet. Come on - we have not another moment to lose! Watson, will you come?'

'Nothing could prevent me!' I cried, delighted to see my friend so animated and excited to observe him in action once again.

Well wrapped in hat, coat, muffler and gloves we climbed into Lestrade's hansom that had been waiting outside. As so often on these occasions Holmes was silent, refusing to answer any of Lestrade's questions, his chin sunk down on his chest, apparently deep in thought. The north-west corner of St James Square was as unlike a crime scene as it was possible for a place to be. A single policeman stood, shivering, outside the formidable building that housed the Library. Aside from that it was a silent, wintery night, the shallow dusting of this morning's snow lending a Christmas feel to it all. Holmes alighted and looked about him in disgust.

'Lestrade - you have been given a unique opportunity in having a crime committed shortly after a snowfall and you allow a whole posse of your policeman to trample over what might have been conclusive evidence. I don't suppose you could have made more of a mess if you had invited onlookers.'

The inspector looked crestfallen but tried a defence. 'I examined the area myself, Mr Holmes. The snow here was already trampled by the people who had used the library all day.'

'I do not doubt that the main pavement was of no service in the detection of footprints, Lestrade, but here in the corner of the square where no pedestrian walks there are the unmistakable imprints of policemen's boots - doubtless looking at the shattered window from what they imagined was the vantage point of the perpetrator and thereby probably obliterating any useful marks forever.

'However, let us hasten inside for this is a bitter night and it may be that you have not yet defaced any evidence there.'

Lestrade looked surprised. 'Inside, Mr Holmes? I have been in the main hall to take a statement from the secretary of the

22

club and I have seen the torn picture with my own eyes to verify the crime but what clues could you possibly hope to find inside?'

A flicker of a smile passed across Holmes' face. 'It is as well to examine the case from all angles. Come, let us enter.'

In the grand, if austere hallway - in keeping with the academic nature of the place - Holmes made straight for the first door on the right that clearly led to the room with the shattered window. Bookshelves from floor to ceiling lined the room apart from at the centre of the near wall - at right angles to the window. Here stood a fireplace and above it hung a large full length portrait of Thomas Carlyle - the Library's founder. An ugly gash, some six to eight inches long, ran left to right bisecting the figure's face with a flap of canvass hanging loose.

'Shocking, isn't it, Mr Holmes,' said Lestrade. All the men who were in here at the time were horrified when they returned from looking out of the window for the culprit when they saw it.'

'How many were there?'

'Some six or seven,' replied Lestrade.

'You have their names. I should like to interview them all.'

'Well, no Mr Holmes. We had no reason to take their particulars. They had nothing more to add to their statements and would have nothing to do with the crime.'

Holmes raised his eyes to the ceiling in despair. 'Were they all members, at least?'

'Oh yes. No guests are admitted to the Library except on guided tours for prospective members and there were none of those today.'

Holmes stood in front of the portrait for some time and gazed at it. Then, without warning, he flung himself on to the floor and regarded the hearth at eye level. Lestrade looked astounded. 'Mr Holmes - I have the champagne cork here of that is what you are looking for.'

But Holmes ignored him and whipped out his magnifying glass to examine the surface of the hearth more closely. He blew over the surface and, seemingly content with the results of his labours, replaced the glass and stood up. Dragging the nearest chair over to the fireplace he climbed on to it to get closer to the gash on the picture. For several minutes he stood motionless, then took out his magnifying glass again and looked afresh. These examinations completed he descended, replaced the chair and again regarded the picture. He raised his stick, as if to point at the gash, and then lowered it. Then he walked over to the window. Here his brow furrowed as he stared out into the gloomy night. Then he turned and made for the door.

'How fortunate that this crime was in the very place in London that is most likely to yield the next clue, inspector. Although I am not a member do you think the secretary would allow me free range amongst the books here for an hour or two?'

'What on earth do you hope to find amongst the books here? I'm sure there would be no objection but what is the point?'

'Ah, just a whim,' smiled Holmes.

For the next hour he roamed the building on his inexplicable quest whilst Lestrade and I chatted in a desultory fashion in the main hall. Finally he emerged from a distant passageway, beaming.

'Well, I think we have achieved all we can here,' he said. 'It is late and I perceive that both of you are tired and ready for bed. Doubtless they wish to lock up the building for the night too.'

'And have you formed any conclusions, Mr Holmes?' asked Lestrade a trifle sarcastically.

Holmes regarded him coldly for a moment. 'Well, despite having made every conceivable error since you embarked upon this case it has still been possible to arrive at several conclusions. Had you called me immediately upon being informed of this incident this evening rather than two hours later I would probably have been able to give you the name and address of the culprit. As it is all I can tell you is that you should seek a man of no more than medium height with square-toed boots who is a member of this library and was here this evening. It is likely he joined only recently. He is also a member of at least two of the other three clubs attacked and visited all of them yesterday evening. I think it is most probable that for the last week or two he has been affecting a leg injury that causes him to carry a stick but this injury is a fake. The stick itself will have a nail or rivet embedded in the handle. He is in financial difficulties. He has an accomplice, probably a family member or close friend, but I have no data on this person as yet other than to say he has an excellent aim. Tomorrow I hope to be able to find the missing pieces of the jigsaw but for now the auctioneers are closed and will not reopen until the morning. Also, I am confident that there will be no more attacks.'

Lestrade had been regarding Holmes with an ever increasing expression of incredulity during the course of this monologue and now exclaimed: 'Come now, Mr Holmes! We know how you like your little games of deduction but this is preposterous. Why should a member of these institutions deface property in his own club? And there is no denying that the windows were broken from the outside. I think you have over-reached yourself this time! Perhaps you are tired?'

Indignation and amusement chased themselves across Holmes' face for a moment.

'I have given you my views, inspector. You go your road; I shall go mine and pursue my own line of investigations. We shall see where they both lead. Come, Watson.'

Without further ado he strode out into the night in search of a hansom cab.

*

On arrival in Baker Street I had retired straight away for I was exhausted and knew from long experience that Holmes would explain himself when he was ready and no amount of cajoling would induce him otherwise. The following morning when I arrived at the breakfast table he was already seated and was studying the papers.

'More news, Holmes?' I enquired.

'That fool Lestrade,' he replied. 'Listen to this piece.
'*In a further development in the case of the vandalised portraits in three St James clubs on Monday night, another identical attack was*

26

made yesterday evening on the London Library damaging their portrait of founder Thomas Carlyle that hangs in the front study. Again a champagne cork was found beneath it.

'Inspector Lestrade, who is leading the investigation, announced late last night that, after questioning, he had released the tramp who had been arrested after the first attack but since then had information about a rowdy group who had dined that night at the Oxford & Cambridge club and left after dinner carrying several bottles of champagne. It is assumed that revelries got out of hand and they seem the likely perpetrators of the outrage. They are helping police with their enquiries.

'He is like a terrier. Once he has a bone he will not let loose. And after all the clues I gave him yesterday evening too. Well, he can chase his own hare. We have a different trail to follow this morning.'

'You are still sure that it was someone inside the clubs?' I asked.

'Is it possible, Watson that you still have not grasped the multitude of clues that we have amassed thus far?'

'I may be very dense, Holmes but I do wish you would explain.'

'Very well. That it could not possibly have been the champagne corks that damaged any of the portraits we demonstrated conclusively during our little outing yesterday. Agreed?'

'Yes.'

'From there it is but a short step to say that the paintings were damaged by someone inside the rooms at the time. I thought it impossible that a guest could gain admittance to all three clubs in the space of two hours - one seemed the maximum. Therefore the culprit must be a member of at least two of them.

'There are probably dozens of men to whom this applies, for being a member of several clubs is not uncommon, but if Lestrade had been the least bit diligent in his workings he would have the name of all those present in the clubs at the time and cross-referencing would have been straightforward. As it is we have to approach the problem another way.

'When I examined the hearth in the London Library there was the mark of the toe of a boot. The wearer had carried in some dirty snow from the square and left a piece behind that had dried. As the fireplace is never used the grate was spotless. One would not light a fire in a room with so many priceless old books in it for the erratic heat would ruin them. Therefore no one would have reason to stand upon this hearth unless to access something above it.'

'That explains your deduction of square-toed boot!' I exclaimed.

'Precisely. But it was only the toe that had left a mark, not the heel. Hence the wearer was standing on tip-toe. You will recall that when I raised my stick to the level of the gash I could reach it easily without stretching. Thus, our criminal is significantly shorter than I am.'

'Outstanding!' I murmured.

'Not at all. So far one could hardly go wrong. Then we come to the gash. You could see that it was at least six inches across. A champagne cork fired at even close range would only cause a very short rent - not six inches! When I examined it close up I could see that it had been made with a blunt point such as a nail or rivet. Therefore I am willing to

28

wager that when we find the culprit he will have an unusual addition to his walking stick.'

'But why do you think he is a young man?'

'Well, when the shot - probably a stone - hit the window naturally everyone's attention would be focused on the smashed pane thus giving our man his opportunity to deface the painting. But he would only have a few seconds before people would look back around the room and he would not want to be seen standing next to the picture. Thus he would have to move fast to rip the painting with his stick, drop a champagne cork and then still be at the window with the rest and so not be suspected. So he would have to be a fairly athletic younger man. In order to be able to carry a walking stick though, he would have to feign a temporary injury necessitating a limp, for all other sticks are left with the porter in the hall.'

'Holmes - you have never risen to greater heights!' I cried.

'I cannot agree,' he replied. 'Even the next step was rather obvious but still Lestrade failed to grasp it. No one has commented much on the four paintings attacked other than to comment that they were of founders of the various institutions. I thought it would be interesting to see if there was any other connection. Fortunately we were in the London Library, which has the capital's largest collection of books on art history. Some patient research gave me the answer: they were all painted by the eminent William Fosdyke RA, who lived from 1795 to 1853.'

'Magnificent! But one moment - didn't Fosdyke paint landscapes? I seem to remember looking at one of his works in the National Gallery only the other week.'

'Excellent, Watson! In one sentence you have put more sense into the case than Lestrade has in two days!' I glowed inwardly with pride.

'You know, I really must give some thought to joining the London Library,' continued Holmes. 'It really is an unmatched store of information. In his later years Fosdyke experimented with other subjects, mostly without much success, but in 1851 he was persuaded to paint his great friends the 2nd Earl of Beauchamp and Thomas Carlyle for the Great Exhibition. The works were an instant success and Fosdyke found himself in great demand for painting others. Beauchamp himself, a great clubman, appears to have suggested that he paint all the founders of the St James clubs, even if the work was from another portrait. This he did starting with the 4th Earl of Aberdeen, a founder member of the Travellers club. Very quickly there was a craze for this and many other founders were petitioning to be next.

'However, it was suggested that as homage to Sir Edward Barnes, the founder of the Army and Navy club who had died only a few years before, he should be the next subject - painted from another portrait that had been done of him by the painter John Wood some year before his death. This was highly acclaimed too and the idea of painting a portrait from another portrait took hold and poor Fosdyke found himself beset on all sides with requests to do just this. Apparently the East India club - only just formed and rather well financed - won this bidding war and so Fosdyke painted Prince Albert, the club's Chief Patron. Again this was highly acclaimed.

'The ensuing rush for his services reached fever pitch but in the midst of it all poor Fosdyke contracted pneumonia and never recovered. So the five paintings were the only portraits he ever painted and they were all in private hands. As you say, he remains best known by the general public for his landscapes.'

'But you said last night that you were confident that no further attacks would occur. Surely the fifth painting is in jeopardy. Shouldn't we inform Lestrade to arrange to have it guarded?'

'No, Watson. For one thing I am disinclined to help Lestrade any further after his insolence last night, and for another I think the painting is safe. We need to consider the motive behind these crimes.'

'I can see nothing obvious.'

'On the contrary, Doctor. The value of the individual paintings was already considerable. Now the fifth - the only undamaged one - will have risen in value phenomenally. Find the owner of the fifth and, if he is in financial trouble, I would suggest you have your man. That is why I am waiting for the auction house to open. I have a contact there who I am sure will be able to furnish us with that missing piece of information. It was the one thing I could not discover in the Library last night.'

'Holmes - you've done it! You solved the case!'

'Not yet, Watson, not yet. We still need the name, link it with a motive, place him at the scene of the crimes, and we also do not know anything more about the accomplice who fired at the windows from outside. There is still much to be done. Can you forgo breakfast for a trip to the auctioneers?'

'Certainly, Holmes!' I cried as nothing gives me more pleasure than to be in at the conclusion of one of my friend's cases - and I sensed the end was close at hand.

The weather was much like the day before. There had been no further snowfall but there was still some fog and the bitter, bitter cold. The horses' breath in the streets billowed out like clouds from a furnace before merging with the misty atmosphere. We hailed a cabby and drove through the icy streets to the auction house, where Holmes introduced me to a small, dapper man in black trousers and tails wearing a golden pince-nez with a very serious expression.

'Watson, this is Dr Cardew - London's foremost authority on art history and retained by all the major auctioneers for his encyclopaedic knowledge on the subject. If anyone can tell us of the history of Fosdyke's portrait of the 2nd Earl of Beauchamp, it is he.'

The little man started and then smiled.

'Mr Holmes, the subject has been the chief topic of conversation in the art world these past two days but not because of the painting's whereabouts - for that is well known - but everyone is curious as to whether it will now be sold for its value is now enormous.'

'Who owns then painting then?' asked Holmes, a little taken aback that someone had more knowledge than he.

'Why - the third earl of course! The portrait has famously never left the family since it was painted.'

Holmes looked surprised again but rallied. 'And you think the value of the remaining intact work is not inconsiderable?'

'Oh yes. Even before these attacks I would have placed a value of twenty thousand pounds on it. But now.... well with this sort of publicity on top of the rarity I imagine it would fetch over fifty thousand at auction if properly handled. We are of course hoping he will sell.'

I was astounded. That any picture could fetch that much money seemed beyond all reason. But Holmes was again spurred into action. He thanked his friend and hastened outside.

'We are on the last lap, Watson,' he said rubbing his hands. 'Could I impose on you to be your guest at your club for ten minutes?' Holmes belonged to no clubs - indeed a less clubbable man would have been hard to find in all London. Even his brother at least belonged to a club for the unclubbable.

'Of course, my dear chap,' I replied. 'To what end?'

'We need to establish whether the Earl of Beauchamp is a member of two of the clubs and of the London Library and further, if he visited these places on Monday and Tuesday nights. Any doorman would remember a personage of such high social standing having visited recently.'

We drove to the East India club. I signed Holmes in at the porter's lodge and we made straight for the library and sought out Burke's peerage. Holmes flicked through the papers impatiently until came to the Earl's entry.

'Here we are: Beauchamp. 3rd Earl.... Hathwick House, Surrey..... Greenfield House, St James..... Ah! look, Watson! Clubs: Travellers, Carlton, East India. Our net draws close! To the porter's desk!'

The stout fellow was keen to be of service.

'Yes, Mr Holmes. His lordship is often here these days. He was certainly here on Monday - and yesterday. I remember for he left shortly after the cork incident. Doubtless he was as upset as the rest of us.' The old man was plainly still rattled after the attack on the institution. His snow-white moustache quivered as he recalled it.

'Thank you, my man,' said Holmes. 'You have been most helpful. Come, Watson. To our next stop. I see our prey has been busy supplying himself with a routine. He visits the club frequently so one more visit is of no great import.'

We walked along the side of the square to the equally imposing Army and Navy club building. As neither of us were members something a little more subtle was called for, but as usual Holmes was up to the task. He approached the porter with a self-deprecating smile. To my surprise he introduced himself as a Mr Cavandish.

'A thousand apologies. I wonder if you can help. I had an appointment here with the Earl of Beauchamp on Monday evening but found myself unavoidably delayed and missed it. It was about a purely business matter. I just wondered if he had left a note for me?'

The porter looked at him I surprise. 'His lordship is not a member here! But as a matter of fact he *was* here on Monday evening. As the guest of a member - perhaps it was the three of you who were to meet?' Holmes nodded vigorously. 'He left quite soon after arriving - I remember thinking it was a short visit at the time. Possibly he could not wait for you, sir. And the poor man - injured and limping as well.' He looked at Holmes somewhat admonishingly as though to scold him for upsetting the plans of such an eminent and disabled person.

'Thank you so much,' replied Holmes stepping briskly out into the street. Outside he turned to me with look of triumph. 'Our theory is looking rather sound, don't you think? Let us see if it holds true for the Travellers.'

We crossed Pall Mall and climbed the steps to the third stage in our quest. Holmes was about to repeat his deception but fortunately the porter interrupted him.

'Why it's Mr Holmes, isn't it? What an honour! I follow all your exploits in the Strand magazine - and is this the good Dr Watson?' I nodded, pleased at also being recognised. 'Are you investigating the disgraceful incident two nights ago? The police do not seem to have made much headway as yet.'

'I am looking into it,' said Holmes. Seizing this lucky chance he leant forward conspiratorially and asked in a low voice: 'Would I be able to see the portrait - with your permission?'

The porter looked delighted. 'Of course, Mr Holmes! Just leave your hat, coat and stick here in the hallway - you too, Doctor - and I'll take you up myself.' He closed up the porter's desk and hurried in front of us along the passage to the front smoking room that faced the street. Holmes followed, seemingly in no hurry.

'What a venerable club, Watson,' he said. 'What a history! And what a building!' The porter, a few steps ahead, seemed delighted. 'I suppose you have you fair share of nobility as members here as well?' continued Holmes. 'Do they frequent the club much too?' he asked innocently.

'Why yes, Mr Holmes,' replied the porter. 'Why just this week the Duke of Wanstead and the Earl of Beauchamp dined here. Two nights ago it was,' he reminisced. 'The day of the incident too,' he went on, looking sad as though the affront had been both to the club's property and to his ability to keep order. 'Here is the portrait.'

Holmes examined it. There was the same six inch gash across the face of the eminent earl. He looked over the hearth but it had been swept clean as this fireplace was in daily use - a cheerful blaze greeted us now. Any marks that may have been there had surely been expunged but Holmes did not seem in the least put out. I guessed that the placing of Beauchamp at the scene for the third time had contented him sufficiently and had been his main goal in coming here. After a little more light conversation with the porter about the event we returned to the entrance hall and struggled back into our coats. Holmes was looking around, puzzled.

'What's wrong, Mr Holmes?' asked the faithful yeoman.

'I had a stick when I came in and placed it here in the stand beneath my hat. It's gone. And we've only been away some ten minutes.'

The porter looked mortified. 'I cannot understand it, sir. No member could possibly have taken it - except by mistake I suppose,' he faltered.

Holmes looked skeptical. 'It was a solid oak cane with a distinctive silver grip. I doubt there are two alike in all London. If someone has taken it - and there would seem to be no other explanation - then they knew full well what they were doing.'

'I shall inform the secretary as soon as he arrives, sir,' wailed the unfortunate porter. 'I'm sure we can retrieve it for you.'

"I cannot share your optimism,' replied Holmes. 'But should the guilty party have a change of heart and return my stick, please send it to 221b Baker Street.' And so saying he turned on his heel and walked out.

'Quite a nest of villainy, wouldn't you say Watson? We have not yet met any members of the club and can already pin five crimes on them! No matter: now for our last port of call.' And he strode off back to St James Square.

The porter at the London Library remembered Holmes from our visit with Lestrade yesterday and naturally assumed that we had simply returned to continue our investigations. Upon being asked he directed us to the offices in the building and then resumed his study of the racing papers. Up in the somewhat less luxurious apartments given over to the administration Holmes immediately sought out the membership secretary - small, dried out old man with a few white tufts of hair sticking out from the side of his head but an otherwise gleaming pate. He was bent over a ledger, totting up figures. Holmes introduced himself with a large degree of deference and asked if he could see a list of new members that had joined in the last year. The old man nodded, perhaps aware that police investigations were still ongoing and much too tired to ask for any formal police identification, wheezed his way to a row of shelves in the far corner of the room and extracted a further ledger with 1895 in gold letters on the spine. This he handed Holmes and promptly collapsed back into his chair as though the effort had been considerable.

Holmes and I eagerly poured over the pages. Each one was dedicated to a new member listing academic qualifications, research interests and referees. The volume was chronological and it was in the June section that Holmes stifled a shout as his long finger pointed to the entry "Lord Beauchamp, 3rd Earl of Beauchamp, joined 20th June, leisure reading."

Holmes snapped the book shut with a grim smile. He handed it back to the old clerk and descended to the main hall, where the porter was still engrossed in the daily papers.

'Is Lord Beauchamp in the Library this morning?' he asked casually.

The porter looked up. 'Bless you - no, sir! He rarely comes in - although he was here a couple of days ago, I recall.'

Holmes took a half-crown out of his pocket and threw it to the man, who caught it deftly and tipped his hat at us as he let us out.'

'Rarely comes in, Watson. Does that not strike you as a little curious for a new member?'

'Almost as if he joined simply for the ability to gain entrance?' I countered following my friend's train of though exactly for once.

'Precisely. Well, we now have him placed at the scene of each crime, we have a possible motive and we have considerable circumstantial evidence. I think it is time we paid a visit to the suspicious earl.'

'You plan to go to his house?' I exclaimed.

'I do. Greenfield House as I recall. From memory it is just round the corner off St James Place.' And he set off at a brisk pace through lifting fog.

Greenfield House, the residence of the Beauchamps for over a century, was the largest building on its street and commanded a view from its rear over the park. Wide steps led up to an imposing portico and black double doors. We pulled on the bell chain and moments later a corpulent butler opened the door and looked at us askance.

'Good morning,' said Holmes affably. 'Sherlock Holmes and Dr Watson. We wish to see Lord Beauchamp.'

'Do you have an appointment?' asked the old retainer dubiously.

'No - but I fancy this will secure us one if you would be so kind as to give it to his lordship.' And he took out one of his cards and scribbled a note on the reverse.

The butler took the card and retreated inside, closing the door.

'What did you write?' I asked curious as to how he has hoped to gain entry.

Holmes smiled. 'I simply wrote *'I would like to return your champagne corks'*. It should suffice, I fancy.'

Sure enough, a few minutes later the door opened and the butler reemerged. 'Please step this way. His lordship is in the drawing room with his daughter.' We entered, although Holmes made a play of stopping to tie his shoelace in the hall, which delayed us almost a full minute.

The butler led the way through a wide corridor lined either side with pictures, although there were several gaps. Holmes nudged me, pointed at these and whispered: 'Selling off the family silver in stages. Financial troubles, you see.' The butler opened the drawing room door and announced us, closing the door behind us.

It was a pleasant room, light and airy, with a blazing fire at one end and a vast tapestry spanning the wall on the other. On a sofa near the fire sat a slim man in his late thirties dressed in a grey suit and reading a book with a child of some eight or nine years. He stood up as we advanced and said: 'Mr Holmes? What is the meaning of this unwelcome intrusion? And what do you mean by your insolent note?' He waved the card at my friend.

Holmes seemed not at all put out by this frosty reception. He walked over to the window and looked over the snowy park. Then he turned and looked keenly at our host.

'I have come to ask you why a respected member of the aristocracy should deface four valuable portraits by the same artist using a nail on the end of a stick in order to raise the value of his own, fifth, painting. Why one would feign an injury necessitating a limp and a walking stick. Why one should join an expensive library and then rarely use it. Why one would arrange a meeting with a friend at a club but leave within half an hour. Indeed, why one would visit three clubs in one evening and not stay more than a few minutes in each. Are your finances so stretched that it has come to this? Was it the Stock Market or cards, sir?'

The earl had turned several shades more red with fury during this string of accusations and finally burst out: 'This is utter nonsense. What possible proof can you have to connect me to all this?'

In answer Holmes held out a stick. 'This, your lordship. Your stick, which I took the liberty of purloining in the hallway just now. It has a nail in the top of the handle. It must be most uncomfortable to use - although I am sure that it will match the gashes in all four paintings exactly.

The sight of his incriminating stick and of Holmes' placid, assured face broke the earl. He staggered back onto the sofa and sat next to his daughter, his head in his hands. At length he spoke.

'How you know this, I cannot fathom - but it is true. I did this. I was desperate. You probably saw the missing paintings as you came along the hall. Several heirlooms - all gone. It was a speculation in South Africa that promised much but was a disaster. These debts have to be paid.'

'A dishonourable course, your lordship.'

'I know, I know,' said the miserable nobleman. 'I was at my wits' end.'

'There is only one thing I do not yet know although it is of little consequence and that is the identity of your accomplice. The man who shot stones at the windows to create the diversion. I would be most obliged if you would let me know. I dislike loose ends in my cases and it will be sure to come out at the trial in any case.'

I have often been amazed by the turn that events took during my time observing cases with Sherlock Holmes but I doubt any took me by quite such surprise as what happened next. The little girl, who had hitherto been sitting silently on the sofa, rose and walked towards Holmes. She looked him full in the face. 'It was I, Mr Holmes. I helped my father.'

Even Holmes, the master of the unexpected himself, was quite taken aback. He recovered his poise with some effort.

'You are the Honourable Lady Caroline Augusta Sophia?'

She nodded.

'And how came you to be such good markswoman?'

'I learnt archery at home in Hathwick House am said to be quite good. I learnt to use a catapult with stones too when papa planned all this.' It was said in all innocence.

Holmes turned to the father. 'You have sunk as low as to involve your own child? Have you no shame?'

But the little girl stood her ground and continued to look straight at Holmes. She was clearly of noble birth. 'No, Mr Holmes. It was my idea. Papa was against it all summer but as things became more desperate he had no choice. I am quite a good shot and a window is a large target.'

As if to prove her statement she went to the far end of the room, opened a drawer and took out a catapult. Then she opened a window, fitted a pebble into the sling and said: 'Look at the wheelbarrow.'

We all turned to look at the object that had been left upended in the garden, half covered in snow. She fired and a loud thud came from the barrow as it shuddered and shed the rest of its snow under impact. She shut the window and turned to face us.

'Mr Holmes. I know what we did was wrong but papa did it for me. If he becomes bankrupt the lawyers will make me live with my mother in Spain. She is a cruel woman and does not like me - and I don't like her either. I want stay here with papa. Please do not give us away.' A tear in the corner of one eye betrayed her straight face but she was too noble to lift a hand to it.

Holmes looked at her thoughtfully. Then he turned to the earl. 'Is this true?' he asked.

'Perfectly true. I wish it were otherwise. When we divorced my wife quickly remarried and so custody of Caroline was given to me on the understanding that if ever I became unable to support her she would be given into the care of her mother.'

There was silence. Holmes turned and walked to the window and looked out for several minutes, deep in thought. When he turned, his eyes too seemed to be glistening somewhat.

'What do you propose to do, Mr Holmes? Will you turn us in?' asked the earl.

'As I had cause to remark to my friend Watson just yesterday I am not retained by the police to make good their deficiencies. Yesterday evening I gave them sufficient clues to guide them but it seems that they are still groping in the dark on a spurious trail. If they were questioning farmers in the Highlands of Scotland they could not be further from the answer and I do not intend to enlighten them.
'However, I presume that you intend to sell the painting and I must insist that out of these profits you must pay for the restoration of the four that you damaged. We were given to understand that the picture would fetch over fifty

thousand pounds so I imagine that there will be plenty left over to pay your debts.

'Furthermore, you must also suffer in some way for the deeds you have committed. You must resign your membership of the East India and Travellers clubs and that of the London Library. You can give any reason you choose.

'You may thank your daughter for my decision, your lordship. Whilst your morals have slipped, she is a remarkable child. Take good care of her.'

For a moment I thought that the earl was also about the shed a tear but he mastered himself, straightened his back and walked over to Holmes to shake his hand.

'God bless you, sir,' he said. 'I shall do all you ask and send the money for repairs as an anonymous donation. You may count on it. I thank you form the bottom of my heart. Is there anything I can do for you? Ask of me what you will and, if it is in my gift, you shall have it.'

'Your lordship does have one item which I would be glad to have and I rather think that you will in any case have little further use for it.'

'You have but to name it.'

'In answer, Holmes held up the stick. 'A memento,' he said. 'I also find that I am, for the moment, without my own.'

If the earl was surprised or relieved or both, he did not show it. 'It is yours,' was all he could say.

Holmes turned to go. At the door however, he paused and turned.